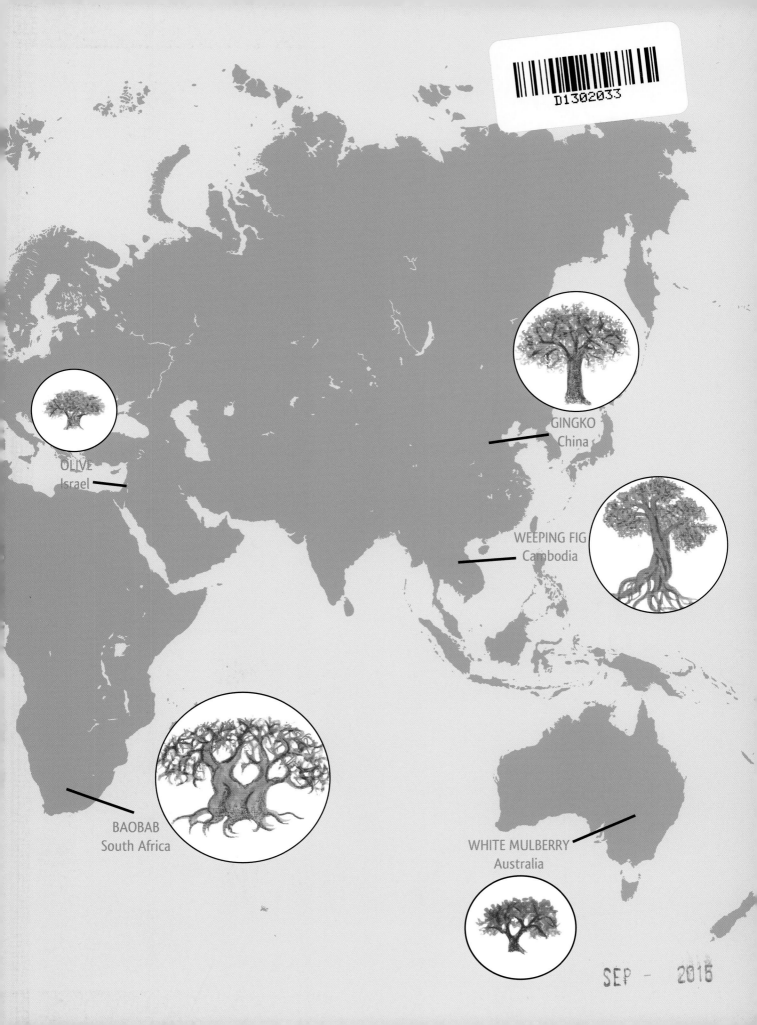

GINGKO
China

WEEPING FIG
Cambodia

OLIVE
Israel

BAOBAB
South Africa

WHITE MULBERRY
Australia

Just Like Me, Climbing a Tree

EXPLORING TREES AROUND THE WORLD

Written & Illustrated by

Durga Yael Bernhard

✤Wisdom Tales✤

Wisdom Tales is an imprint of World Wisdom, Inc.

Library of Congress Cataloging-in-Publication Data

Bernhard, Durga, author, illustrator.
 Just like me, climbing a tree : exploring trees around the world / written & illustrated by Durga Yael Bernhard.
     pages cm
  Audience: Ages 4-8.
  Audience: K to grade 3.
  ISBN 978-1-937786-34-2 (hardcover : alk. paper) 1. Trees--Juvenile literature. 2. Tree climbing--Juvenile literature. 3. Ecology--Juvenile literature. I. Title.
  QK475.8.B48 2015
  582.16--dc23
                                                                              2014040810

Printed in China on acid-free paper

Production Date: November 2014, Plant & Location: Printed by 1010 Printing International Ltd,
Job/Batch #: TT14100778

For information address Wisdom Tales, P.O. Box 2682,
Bloomington, Indiana 47402-2682
www.wisdomtalespress.com

For James & Alma;
and for Victoria —
who loves to climb trees

What if you
heard a bird
in the branches above,

and your feet
followed a root...

WEEPING FIG
ficus benjamina
Cambodia

or you shimmied up a trunk
so thick and tough,

and swung
like monkeys do?

MONTEZUMA CYPRESS
taxodium mucronatum
Mexico

MANGO
mangifera indica
Guinea, West Africa

Then you leaped to a limb
like a leopard,
and balanced on a bough,

MONTEREY PINE
pinus radiata
California

or spotted a spider
spinning a web,

and hung like a bat
upside down?

What if you crept

like a
chameleon
along a crack,

and knew
about a nest,

BAOBAB
adansonia digitata
South Africa

LYCHEE
litchi chinensis
Hawaii

and reached for the very ripest fruit
and tasted some of the best?

What if you caught
a caterpillar eating a leaf

WEEPING WILLOW
salix babylonica
Holland

and dodged a dragonfly?

Or you slept like a sloth
in the canopy,

then watched with
an eagle's eye?

KAPOK
ceiba pentandra
Brazil

OLIVE
olea europaea
Israel

Or you found
a hidden hollow
where you could
tuck your treasures,

then you sat
in the shade,
listened to leaves,
and felt the
changing weather?

GINGKO
gingko biloba
China

WHITE MULBERRY
morus alba
Australia

What if you spotted
a slinky silkworm,
and wanted to climb again?

SOUTHERN LIVE OAK
quercus virginiana
Southeast United States

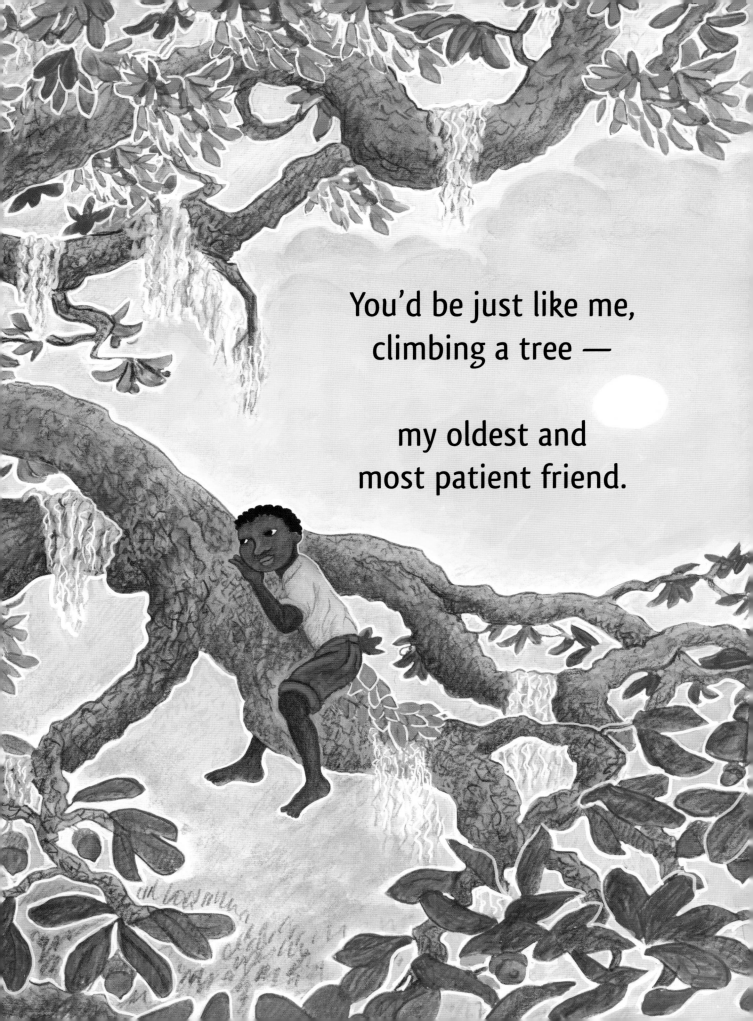

You'd be just like me,
climbing a tree —

my oldest and
most patient friend.

About the Trees in This Book

WEEPING FIG
ficus benjamina
Cambodia

There are many kinds of fig trees, ranging from the common fica that lives in indoor pots, to weeping figs with massive snake-like roots, to banyans with branches that grow downward to form multiple trunks, or "pillar roots." Most fig trees live in the tropical forests of India, Asia, and northern Australia. The fig tree found in the Bible is native to the Middle East, and the only one with lobed (wavy-edged) leaves. The weeping fig has narrow, glossy leaves; dramatic, twisting branches; and powerful roots that can strangle other trees, crack walls, and lift up sidewalks. Its dark red fruit is an important food for many animals and birds, including parrots, pigeons, and doves. Fig flowers grow inside the fruit sac which must be pollinated by a tiny "gall" wasp that lays its eggs inside the sac. Each type of fig attracts its own special wasp.

MONTEZUMA CYPRESS
taxodium mucronatum
Mexico

The Montezuma cypress is a large evergreen that grows along rivers, springs, and marshes in the highlands of Mexico. Outside its native area, the tree becomes deciduous, dropping its needles in winter. The Montezuma cypress is sacred to the native peoples of Mexico, and as part of their creation myths is thought to have special powers. Its wood resists moisture and is used for large house beams, fences, and outdoor furniture. The bark and resin are used for making medicines. The famous "Tule Tree" of Oaxaca, Mexico, also called "El Gigante," is thought to be over 2,000 years old. It has the second thickest tree trunk in the world. In 1520, the Spanish explorer Hernán Cortés wrote about this very same tree! But scientists today believe the Tule Tree may actually be three cypress trees that have grown together to form a single trunk.

MANGO
mangifera indica
Guinea, West Africa

Mango trees are native to South Asia, but they are widely grown as an important food source all over the tropics. This popular evergreen has been cultivated for over 4,000 years, and is the subject of many stories, poems, and songs. The paisley pattern used in decorative art for centuries is based on the shape of an Indian mango. Young mango trees produce dark red leaves. Mature trees have dark green leaves and a lush, broad crown that often becomes a shady place for people in hot climates to gather. Mango trees have a deep taproot that makes it tolerant of poor shallow soil. The leaves, sap, and skin can cause a skin rash in some people. The tasty fruit pulp is rich in minerals and vitamins, and can be blended, chopped, pickled, preserved, dried, or made into sauces, ice cream, or smoothies.

MONTEREY PINE
pinus radiata
California

The Monterey pine is native to the coast of California and Mexico. It is a fast-growing coniferous evergreen that is resistant to coastal winds and thrives in rocky places. The wild tree grows up to 100 feet tall; its low branches and broad, twisted shape make the tree look like it's dancing in the wind. The modern cultivated tree can grow twice as tall, and if pruned to grow straight, produces good lumber and valuable pulp for making paper. The cones of the Monterey pine are adapted to open in high temperatures so that the tree will reseed itself readily after a fire. Monterey pines are a host for the mistletoe plant, and a favorite food of goats, which can climb the trees and if left unchecked, can cause a lot of damage. Certain groves of Monterey pine along the Pacific Ocean have also become important wintering habitat for the migrating monarch butterfly.

BAOBAB
adansonia digitata
South Africa

Known as the elephant of trees, this giant of the African savannah can live for over 1,000 years and grow to over 60 feet high. The baobab is home to many birds, including the yellow hornbill, orange-bellied parrot, and buffalo weaver. Its smooth gray bark is eaten by elephants, and its leaves are nibbled by tall giraffes. Its fluffy white flowers are full of nectar that is gathered by brown bats, furry mammals called bushbabies, and grazing antelopes. Its pulpy fruit is eaten by baboons, and its thick limbs provide cover for leopards. But for most of the year, the twisting, crooked branches of the baobab are bare, making the tree look like it is planted upside down with its roots in the air!

LYCHEE
litchi chinensis
Hawaii

Lychees are native to China and Malaysia, and are now grown in many tropical and subtropical parts of the world. They are evergreen trees that can grow up to 50 feet tall, but are typically shorter and easy to climb. Lychee trees are grown for their ornamental beauty as well as for the fruit. The leaves of the lychee tree are almost waterproof, and provide good shelter for birds. The fruit has a white, edible pulp inside with a sweet flavor and a fragrant smell that is lost in canning, so it is most popular eaten fresh. Dried lychees are called lychee "nuts," even though they are fruits. Wild lychee trees still dominate the tropical rainforests of southern China. The fruit is a favorite food of lorikeets (a kind of parrot) and fruit bats, which can easily wipe out a lychee grower's crop, so many growers cover their trees with nets. The lychee tree is a symbol of romance because most people quickly fall in love with the exotic perfume of the fruit the first time they taste it!

WEEPING WILLOW
salix babylonica
Holland

There are over 300 types of willows, ranging from small shrubs to tall trees. Weeping willows are native to China, where they have long been grown as ornamental trees and for protection from wind. Willows grow rapidly near rivers, streams, swamps, and lakes, but their lifespan is short for a tree: only 40 to 75 years. Their roots can be very aggressive in seeking water, and have been known to damage pipes, sewers, and building foundations. Willows bloom early in the spring, with flowers arranged in "catkins" — clusters that hang in long strands. Male and female catkins grow on separate trees. Willow wood is resistant to fire and has been used for making baskets, boxes, cricket bats, tool handles, and railway parts. Willow branches are tough and elastic and make excellent "bentwood" furniture. Many insects, birds, and animals eat willow leaves, branches, and bark. Willow bark contains salicin, a substance that was first used for making aspirin.

KAPOK
ceiba pentandra
Brazil

The kapok, ceiba, or "silk cotton" tree of Central and South America has a huge, thick trunk with buttressed roots and heavy branches that often grow straight out to the side. Known as an "emergent" tree, the kapok can grow up to 230 feet high, often rising above the canopy of tropical rainforests, where it is bathed in sunlight, enabling the growth of a broad crown. Young kapok trees produce spiny cones on their trunks that make the tree difficult to climb. Older kapoks create shade and shelter for many birds and animals, including monkeys, sloths, harpy eagles, toucans, snakes, and porcupines. The kapok tree is deciduous, shedding all its leaves in the dry season. This gives the trees beneath it a chance to receive more sunlight. Its fruit pods contain a fluffy fiber that has been used to stuff mattresses, pillows, life jackets, and stuffed toys. The seeds are used in soap and also make good fertilizer. The kapok tree was sacred to the Mayan people and an important source of healing medicine. They believed a departing soul could ascend to heaven by rising up the trunk of a great mythical kapok tree.

OLIVE
olea europaea
Israel

The olive tree is an evergreen, short and gnarly with a fruit called a "drupe." It is native to the Mediterranean, but is now cultivated as far away as India, New Zealand, and California. The olive tree has played a major role in shaping human history. Its oil has been used to worship gods, dedicate temples, light up palaces, anoint kings, and beautify queens. Throughout recorded history, olive groves have been both refuges of peace and places of war. These unique trees are dependent upon humans in order to thrive. With proper pruning, they can live for thousands of years. As olive trees age, they develop many folds and hollows which sometimes resemble a face, giving each tree a unique character. Even after burning to the ground, an olive tree has the ability to regenerate a new trunk, thus making it a symbol of peace and renewed life. Perhaps this is why the dove that Noah sent out from the ark at the end of the great biblical flood returned with an olive branch.

GINGKO
gingko biloba
China

The gingko tree, also known as the maidenhair tree, is one of the oldest trees known to humanity, dating back to the time of dinosaurs. Gingko trees are native to China and venerated by many Buddhists and Taoists in parts of Asia. Gingko is resistant to insects, pollution, and disease, enabling many trees to live as long as 2,000 years. Some gingko trees even survived the atomic bombing in Hiroshima, Japan in 1945. Gingko grows well in soil that is disturbed, so it thrives in cities, where the tree is prized for its shade, its unique fan-shaped leaves, and its lovely golden autumn foliage. Older gingko trees are capable of sprouting aerial roots which enable the tree to reproduce by cloning. Cloning male gingko trees is a popular alternative to reproduction by seeds, as the female gingko tree produces a foul-smelling flower. The nut-like seeds are considered a delicacy in Chinese and Japanese cuisine, and the leaves have long been used for making medicine. Today, gingko trees are found on city streets in Asia, Europe, and North America.

WHITE MULBERRY
morus alba
Australia

Mulberries are deciduous trees that thrive in the tropics, but have also been cultivated in temperate climates — especially China and Persia, where silk was first produced from silkworms that feed exclusively on the leaves of the white mulberry. Ancient trade routes to the Orient were thus named the "Silk Road." Mulberry trees are also useful in other ways: the stems produce a milky sap that contains latex. The bark of the tree contains substances that are being studied for producing powerful medicines, and the fruit contains dyes that are used to make natural food coloring. The wood is prized for building furniture. The foliage has been used for feeding cattle. In North America, mulberry fruits were an important source of food for native Americans and early explorers. In Australia, mulberry trees were successfully introduced by English settlers in the 1830s, some of which are still growing today and have become historical landmarks.

SOUTHERN LIVE OAK
quercus virginiana
Southeast United States

The southern live oak is a massive tree that thrives in the southern United States. During colonial times, it was planted on plantations and farms for its shade and beauty, and for grazing pigs and chickens that fed on its acorns. Many of those trees still stand today. The southern live oak is resistant to wind, floods, and fire, making it a good shelter for migrating and nesting birds. The wood is so strong that it is used to build the hulls of ships. Unlike other oaks, the southern live oak does not shed its leaves in winter, thus appearing alive all year round and earning its name. It has a short trunk and long branches which often sweep downward to almost touch the ground before curving up again, making it an excellent climbing tree. Spanish moss and ferns often hang from its branches, giving the tree a uniquely southern appearance. Famous southern live oaks such as the "Seven Sisters Oak" (in Louisiana) and the "Angel Oak" (in South Carolina) may be visited from Florida to Texas.

Why You Should Be
Careful When Climbing Trees

• Climbing should be fun, and getting hurt or stuck is no fun! Some branches are too weak to hold you, or they might be slippery. Sometimes it is harder to get down than it is to climb up! Always ask an adult before you climb a tree.

• Trees can be hurt, too. Breaking branches or stripping off bark can cause harm, and that's not fun for the tree!

• Birds and other animals rest in trees or make their homes there. For your safety and theirs, don't disturb those who are sharing the tree with you.

 For more information about trees and how this book was made:

• Visit D. Yael Bernhard's book blog at dyaelbernhard.com/bookblog for a post about this book with lots more information from the author and illustrator.

• Look on the internet or in a "field guide" book to help you identify the kinds of trees that you see around you. The Arbor Day Foundation website has many good resources on trees, educational programs, and much more.

• The Wisdom Tales website has a page on *Just Like Me, Climbing a Tree*, with links to activities such as coloring pages, a discussion guide for classroom use, and more.

 Just Like Me Song

• There is a song about this book! It is written and sung by award-winning children's performer Story Laurie (Laurie McIntosh). You can download the song at www.storylaurie.com/just-like-me. It is a wonderful support for children at home or school who are reading the book.